Rosie Sprout's
Time
to
Shine

story by
Allison Wortche

pictures by
Patrice Barton

Alfred A. Knopf

New York

Violet was the best — everyone agreed.

She ran the fastest in gym class.

She sang the highest in choir practice.

She was the loudest storyteller at lunchtime.

And she looked the fanciest on picture day.

Violet was definitely the best. And everyone agreed.

Except Rosie.

Rosie was not a fast runner.

She could not sing very high.
  She was not the loudest storyteller.

And she did not get very fancy for picture day.

But Rosie was tired of hearing about Violet being the best.

One morning, Ms. Willis told the class they would each grow their own pea plants in little pots on the windowsill in the back of the classroom. Everyone was excited.

Violet was the most excited. Her plant would definitely be the tallest. (She *was* the best, after all.)

For homework, the students had to decorate their pots.
"Plants like nice places to grow," Ms. Willis said.

Violet's pot was the sparkliest. Rosie's wasn't.
But it still seemed like a nice place to grow.

As Ms. Willis helped the students put soil into their
pots, she asked, "What do seeds need to become
healthy plants?"

Ms. Willis was impressed. "What good gardeners you all are!"

Rosie made a hole in the soil with her finger, dropped in a little seed, and carefully covered it up.

air

soil

water

sunlight

Days went by, and everyone waited. They watered their pots, but nothing happened.

Then one afternoon, Rosie noticed a green dot poking through her soil. There was a tip of green in Violet's pot, too. Rosie couldn't wait to show Ms. Willis.

But Violet, who was the fastest, yelled, "Mine is the first to grow! Hooray!"

The next morning, Rosie got to school early to check on her plant. She was very proud of it. But Violet's was a little bigger than hers. *It figures,* Rosie thought.

She looked over her shoulder. No one was there yet except Ms. Willis, who was writing vocabulary words on the chalkboard.

seed
root
stem
sprout
leaf
nutrients

Bonus words!

oxygen
carbon dioxide
chlorophyll
photosynthesis

Quickly, Rosie pushed the soil on top of Violet's plant. *There,* she thought. *Now* my *plant is the best.* She slid into her seat.

Rosie felt like "the best" for a few seconds. Then she started to feel a little guilty. But the bell rang, and she knew it was too late to fix things.

When everyone was seated, Rosie noticed that Violet wasn't there.

Rosie slinked down in her chair. She'd started out feeling bad for Violet's plant. Now she was feeling a little bad for Violet, too. Just a little. She knew what she had to do.

For the next two weeks, Rosie came to school early and took care of *two* plants.

She gently shook off the soil she'd pushed on top of Violet's little sprout.

She watered her plant, and she also watered Violet's.

Rosie S.
watering chart
Monday: my plant ✓
            Violet's plant ✓
Tuesday: mine ✓
            Violet's ✓
Wednesday: my peas ✓
              Violet's peas
...sday: me
        Violet ✓
...riday: me ✓
        Violet ✓

She sang quiet little songs about growing to her plant,
and then she sang to Violet's.

She made sure they were both in the bright sunlight.

Ms. Willis was very pleased. "I believe you're the best gardener I've ever had, Rosie! Yes, *definitely* the best!"
Rosie beamed.

When Violet finally returned to school, everyone crowded around to hear about her chicken pox.

"My doctor told me I had the *worst* case of chicken pox he'd *ever* seen!"

It wasn't long before Violet remembered about her pea plant. When she skipped to the back of the classroom, everyone followed.

"My plant is the tallest! Hooray!" Violet exclaimed happily.

Then she noticed the one next to hers. "Whose is that?"

"That's Rosie's. She's been taking such good care of *both* plants," Ms. Willis told the class. Everyone agreed—Violet's and Rosie's plants were the tallest.

"Thanks, Rosie," Violet said very quietly.
  "Well," she said much louder as everyone returned to their seats, "mine's still the sparkliest!"

Ms. Willis looked at Rosie. Rosie looked at Ms. Willis.
And they smiled.

For my mom, dad, and sister, with love.
And for my many inspiring teachers,
with gratitude. —A.W.

For my sweet aunt Judy. —P.B.

THIS IS A BORZOI BOOK PUBLISHED BY ALFRED A. KNOPF

Text copyright © 2011 by Allison Wortche
Jacket art and interior illustrations copyright © 2011 by Patrice Barton

All rights reserved. Published in the United States by Alfred A. Knopf,
an imprint of Random House Children's Books, a division of Random House,
Inc., New York.

Knopf, Borzoi Books, and the colophon are registered trademarks of
Random House, Inc.

Visit us on the Web! www.randomhouse.com/kids

Educators and librarians, for a variety of teaching tools, visit us at
www.randomhouse.com/teachers

Library of Congress Cataloging-in-Publication Data
Wortche, Allison.
Rosie Sprout's time to shine / story by Allison Wortche ;
pictures by Patrice Barton. — 1st ed.
p. cm.
Summary: Rosie's rival, Violet, outdoes her in everything until the class plants
seeds for a unit on gardening.
ISBN 978-0-375-86721-7 (trade) — ISBN 978-0-375-96721-4 (lib. bdg.)
[1. Schools—Fiction. 2. Competition (Psychology)—Fiction. 3. Plants—Fiction.]
I. Barton, Patrice, ill. II. Title.
PZ7.W887837Ro 2011
[E]—dc22
2011004092

The illustrations in this book were created using pencil
sketches painted digitally.

MANUFACTURED IN CHINA
December 2011
10 9 8 7 6 5 4 3 2 1

First Edition